The Lion King

A Giant Leap

A WELCOME BOOK

NEW YORK

With special thanks to the hundreds of animators, artists, and craftspeople at the Walt Disney Studios whose extraordinary work fills the pages of this book.

The producer would also like to thank the following for their generous assistance:

Don Hahn

Lella Smith, Vivian Procopio, and Ann Hansen of the Disney Feature Animation Research Library

For information address Disney Editions
114 Fifth Avenue, New York, New York 10011-5690
www.disneyeditions.com

Produced by Welcome Enterprises, Inc.,
6 West 18 Street, New York, New York 10011
www.welcomebooks.biz

Disney Editions Editorial Director: Wendy Lefkon
Disney Editions Assistant Editor: Jody Revenson
Designed by H. Clark Wakabayashi

Library of Congress
Cataloging-in-Publication Data on file

ISBN 0-7868-5393-X

Printed in Singapore
First Edition
1 3 5 7 9 10 8 6 4 2

Contents

Introduction

DON HAHN

Making an animated film, or any film for that matter, is a leap of faith. There's nothing to guarantee that the years of passion that get poured out onto the screen will amount to anything that an audience will want to see. When it does, it's fairly astounding. The history of *The Lion King* is fairly astounding

The idea for an African story told with lions had been in development at the studio since 1989 in various forms and under various titles. Some early versions read like a dusty African homage to *Bambi.* Some featured characters like Simba's little brother Meetoo, or a bat-eared fox named Bahti. After three years, hundreds of sketches, thousands of script pages, and a research trip to Africa, the clear story of Simba had still not emerged.

Then came a pivotal few days in early 1992 when the fog lifted. That's when directors Rob Minkoff, Roger Allers, and I locked ourselves into an office in our warehouse studio with *Beauty and the Beast* directors Kirk Wise and Gary Trousdale, Brenda Chapman-Lima, and a lot of paper and pizza. Two days later, a compelling story began to emerge: it was a love story between a father and his son—a love story that grew stronger even in death.

As the story grew, the next panic came when the animators realized that they hadn't animated four-legged characters in years. It was time to go to school. We brought live lions into the studio. Animators traveled to the L.A. Zoo almost weekly to study the finer points of warthog locomotion, or meerkat anatomy. All this homework came back to the studio in the form of animation tests and experiments to show how this story could be told with a cast of characters that walked on four legs and had no opposable thumb.

Animation is a medium that combines

equal parts art, allegory, and alchemy. There is by nature nothing real about what we as filmmakers put on the screen. Yet somehow the ingredients of pencil, paper, pixels, and phosphor all combine in a craft that can put across very powerful emotions—emotions that feel very real to us even though they come from on-screen actors that are lions, meerkats, and warthogs.

Hard work and preparation can get you to a point, but then there are those days when fate steps in to indicate the direction. Like the day Nathan Lane and Ernie Sabella came in to audition as hyenas at a New York casting call. After they had left the room and the auditions had moved on to the next actor, Nathan and Ernie asked if they could come back and read a scene together as a team. It worked. So much so that the directors cast them not as hyenas, but as the now famous duo: Timon and Pumbaa.

Another fateful day: Hans Zimmer had done a stirring arrangement of the Elton John–Tim Rice anthem "The Circle of Life," but something was missing. We all knew that to establish the African setting, we wanted a more indigenous sound from the very first frame of film. Hans asked us over to his studio one night. His office was stacked with old guitars. In the corner a table was laden with audiotapes and Chinese food. It was on that night, in that backroom studio, where Lebo M experimented with ways to start the film. After a few takes, seemingly out of nowhere came the now famous cry in the wilderness that begins *The Lion King*.

No one could have imagined that this coming-of-age story about a lion cub that gets framed for murder would amount to much. In the early days of production, I had trouble getting people to work on the film. At times when *The Lion King* was at full throttle, we started to wonder what we had done, or if anyone would want to see it. I remember calling my sister and telling her I was working on a film about a lion cub and his friends, a meerkat and a flatulent warthog. It was, "sort of Moses and Joseph meet Elton John and Hamlet in Africa," I said. There was a very long pause on the other end of the line. Then she said: "Well, I hope it works out." It did.

From its inception under the title *King of the Jungle*, to long hours at the drawing board, to opening night at Radio City Music Hall, to the record-setting box-office success, to the Broadway musical inspired by the film, *The Lion King* has become, by anyone's definition, a phenomenon.

When Susan Wloszczyna, film critic for *USA Today*, wrote recently about the ten films that defined the term "blockbuster," she wrote, of course, about *Star Wars* and *Jaws*, but she also included *The Lion King* as the film that established a new genre: the animated blockbuster.

Cut to: eight o'clock on an early June morning in 2002. A group of about a hundred of the original filmmakers gathered to drink coffee, eat doughnuts, and watch the large-format version of *The Lion King* for the first time. What we saw was fairly astounding.

The Lion King was one of the earliest films to be completed in a digital format using Disney's own Academy Award–winning production system. This meant that back in 1994, each of the finished scenes in the film was stored as a digital file burned on CD (much like you would burn a CD on your home computer). When it came time to prepare the film for its large-screen debut, the team took the original data from each scene in the film and doubled the resolution of each image. The individual frames were then printed on 70mm large-format film stock and checked for quality.

At the same time, dozens of scenes were redrawn or digitally retouched to help the film play in this new giant format. The sound track also got a digital tune-up to prepare for the spectacular sound configuration of large-format and Imax theaters.

After a year of careful digital restoration, remastering, and reprinting, and after about a decade of unimaginable events, we sat in a huge Imax theater that June morning and did what we had always hoped the audience would do: we were swept away by the art, allegory, and alchemy of animation and the many wonders of a very special love story—*The Lion King*.

TOP: *A Burbank audience views the large-screen format of* The Lion King.

MIDDLE AND BOTTOM: *Samples in actual size of 70mm film (from* The Lion King) *and traditional 35mm motion picture film (from* Fantasia 2000)

The Lion King

In the velvet blackness of an African night,
at the hour before dawn when the land is full of dreams,
a lone voice heralds the new day.

As the red disk of the sun rises,
the one voice becomes many
until the Pride Lands echo with song.

The distant mountain floats above the mist.
Vast herds move across the golden plain,
and the heavens come alive with storks and doves,
kingfishers, and flamingos.

High on Pride Rock, Mufasa the Lion King waits,
watching as the creatures of his domain gather below
to celebrate the arrival of the newborn prince.

Rafiki, keeper of the mysteries,
anoints Prince Simba's brow,
sprinkles the cub with ceremonial dust,
and raises him to the skies
for all of heaven and earth to see.

Mufasa's jealous sibling, Scar,
sits in the shade, taking bitter pride in his absence
from the sacred ceremony, scheming and dreaming of the day
he will usurp the throne.

Zazu the hornbill, Pride Rock's chief of protocol,

informs an indifferent Scar

his truancy has not gone unnoticed.

Confronted by Mufasa,

Scar hides his rage beneath a cloak of scorn.

Each sunrise finds Simba in the royal cave,
nudging his father from sleep, begging him to join
in the immemorial games that ensure
the survival of the species.

From the peak of Pride Rock,
father and son survey the Lion King's domain.

Crossing his kingdom, Mufasa speaks earnestly
of the Circle of Life—the endless chain
that links all living things,
from the crawling ant to the leaping antelope.

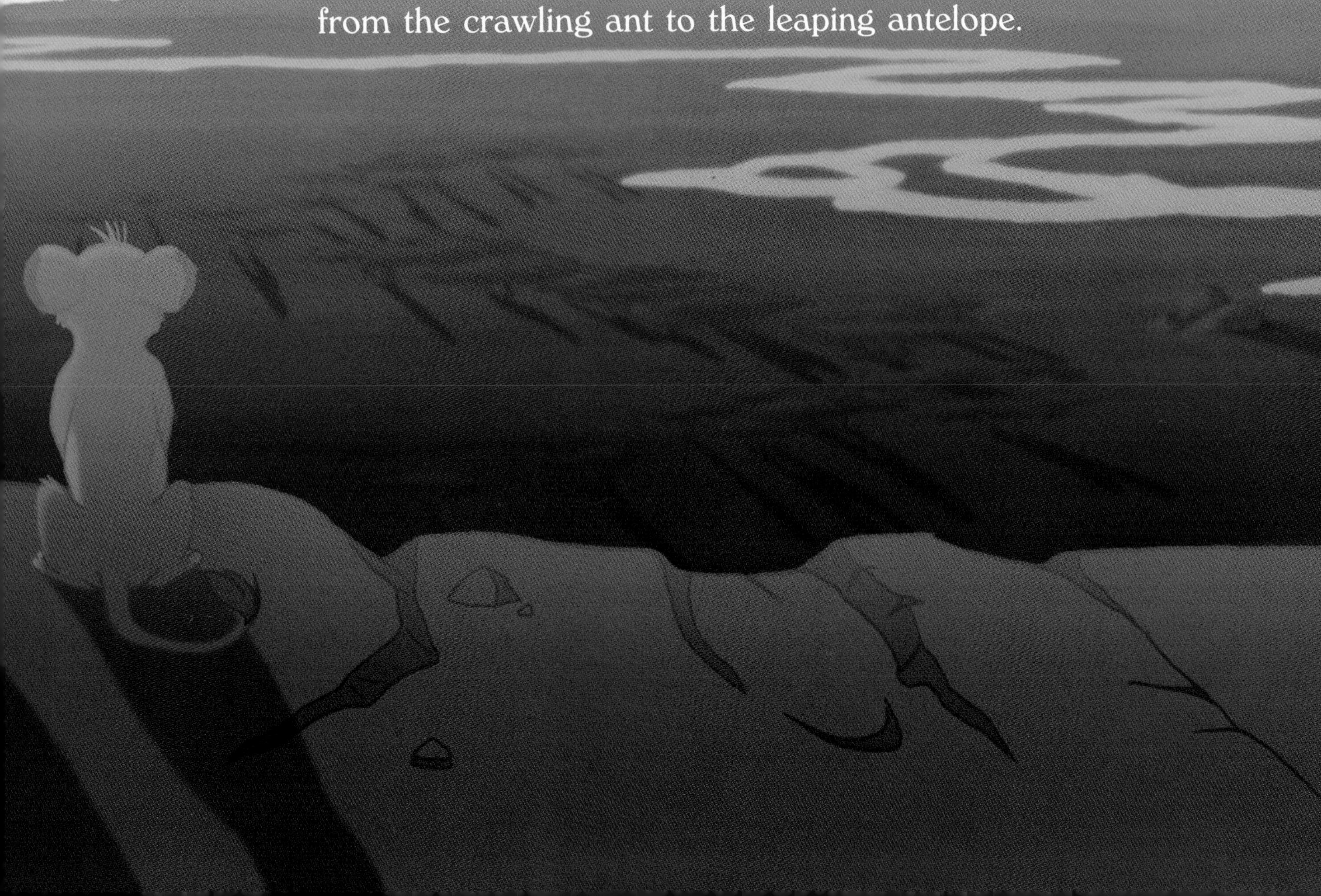

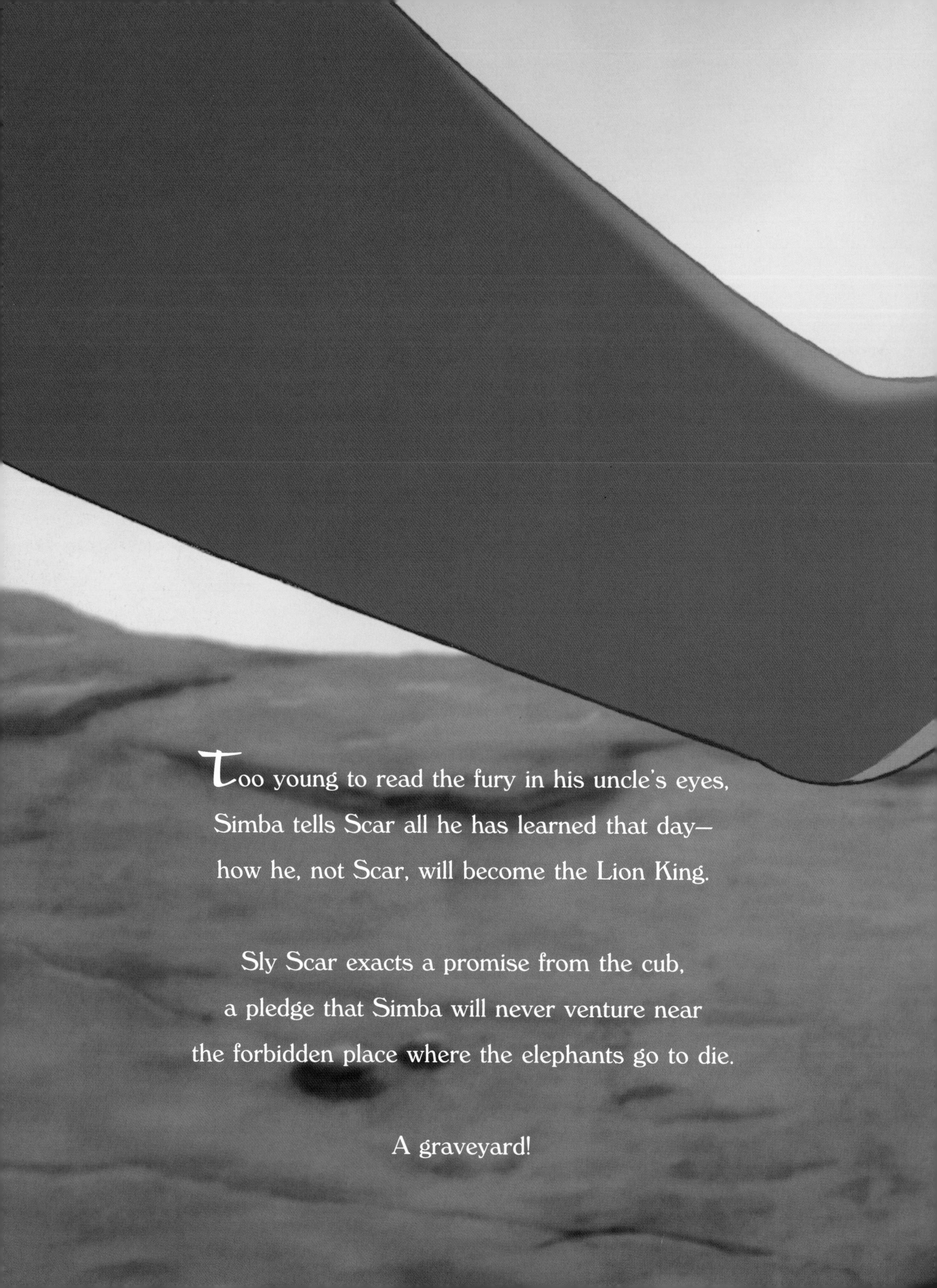

Too young to read the fury in his uncle's eyes,
Simba tells Scar all he has learned that day—
how he, not Scar, will become the Lion King.

Sly Scar exacts a promise from the cub,
a pledge that Simba will never venture near
the forbidden place where the elephants go to die.

A graveyard!

Scar has planted a secret Simba must share at once with Nala, his greatest and most trusted friend.

He finds her in the dappled shade of Pride Rock,
lazing with the lionesses of the pride.

Simba and Nala can barely mask their curiosity,
but first they must lose their escort, Zazu,
sent along to keep mischief at bay.

Mistaking the cubs' whispered plans for love talk,

Zazu imagines that romance is blooming.

The cubs scoff at his quaint ideas

and plot their escape.

Trying to elude their feathered guardian,
the cubs play hide-and-seek.

Elephants and hippos, monkeys and giraffes
join in the fun as Simba sings his song.

"I'm going to be

a mighty king!”

Escaping Zazu,
the lion cubs arrive at the graveyard,
an eerie spot guarded by thermal springs.

A jet of steam subsides to reveal an eerie landscape littered with skeletons and monumental piles of bones. This macabre world seems to go on forever, vanishing into hissing vapor and eternal gloom.

From within a massive skull comes chilling laughter,
and in the empty sockets blazing eyes appear.
A grinning trio of hyenas slinks into view:
Baleful Shenzi, sadistic Banzai, and addlepated Ed.

Weaving amongst the skeletons, blinded by mist and steam,
their short legs racing over treacherous terrain,
Simba and Nala flee, hyenas in pursuit.

Zazu is caught
and plunged into a thermal cauldron,
barely escaping with his feathers intact.

A roar seems to bring the whole world to a stop.
The three hyenas freeze
until Mufasa's paw sends them running.

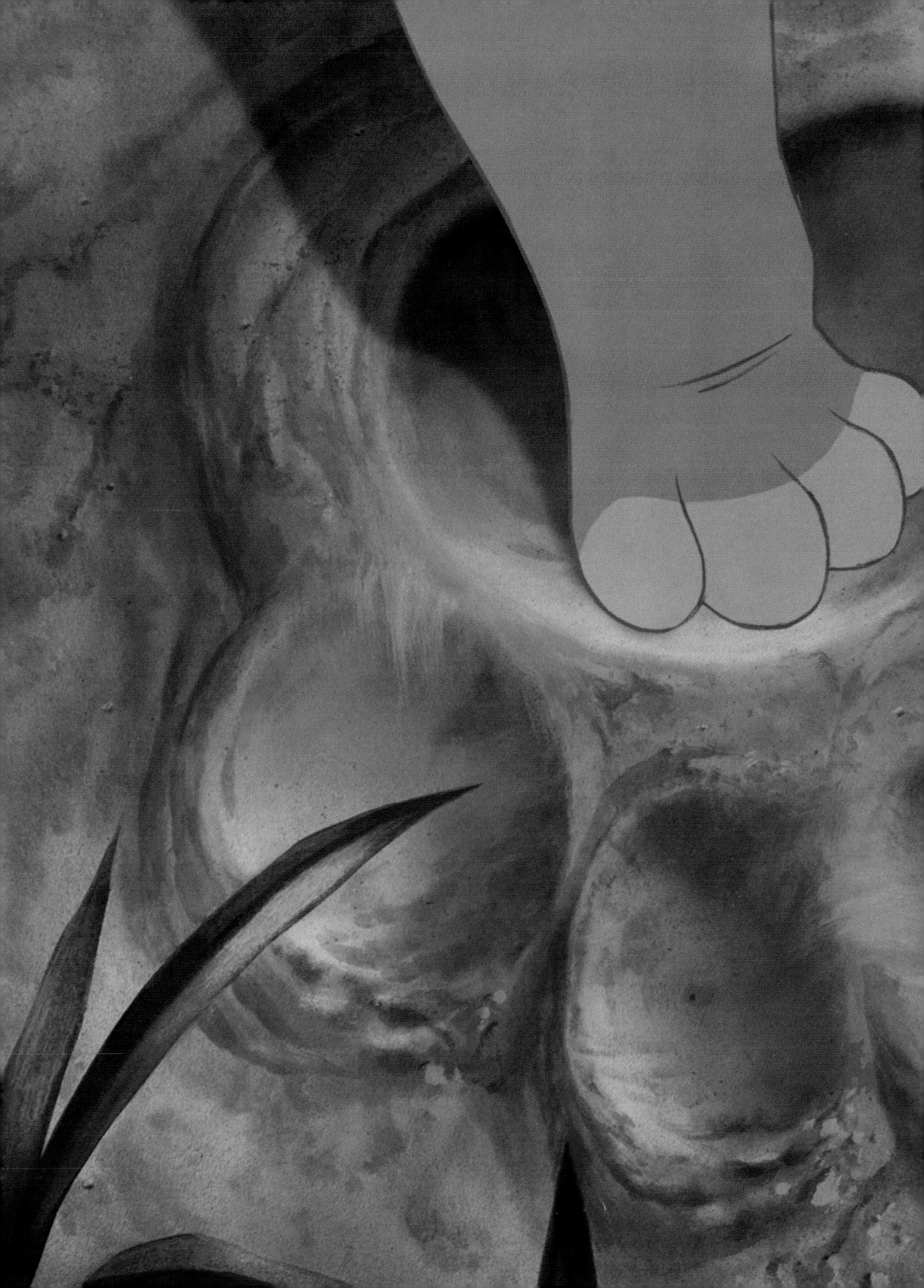

The sun sinks in the sapphire sky,
but Simba does not notice its expiring glory.
His head hung in shame, he follows Mufasa home,
planting his childish paws in his father's giant footsteps.

In the gathering dusk, Mufasa turns to face his son.
Tears of regret glisten in Simba's eyes.

Mufasa talks of wisdom and folly,
the difference between bravery and bravado,
and explains how even a Lion King can know fear
when he believes he may have lost a son he loves.

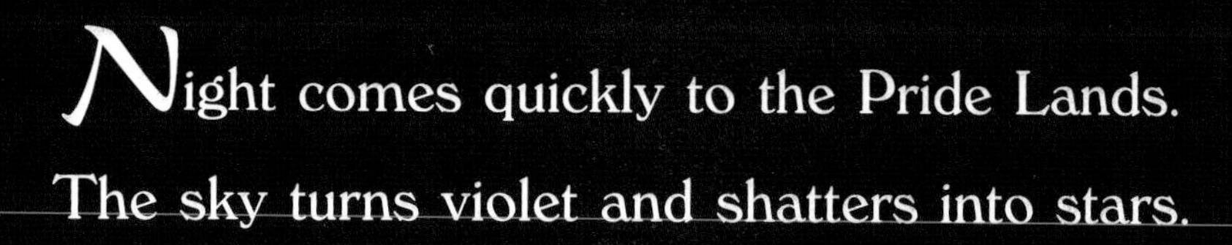

Night comes quickly to the Pride Lands.
The sky turns violet and shatters into stars.
At this magic hour, Mufasa and his son
sit beneath the slowly turning galaxies,
surrendering themselves to
the rhythms of the nocturnal world.

Mufasa passes along the wisdom of the pride,
telling Simba how the great kings of the past
look down from the stars and will always be there
to guide him.

Meanwhile, Scar conceives a bolder scheme,
one that will rid the Pride Lands of King Mufasa
and the royal brat at one fell swoop.
Scar preens and poses on his rocky pedestal,
exhorting his accomplices to greater heights of infamy.

Rank upon rank of hyenas strut below
as geysers erupt in clouds of steam.
The earth itself appears to crack apart
in the face of Scar's villainous ambitions.

With lies and wily flattery,
Scar lures Simba to a winding gorge
and tells him to wait there until Mufasa comes.

As Simba practices his roar,
Scar signals to his criminal confederates
and sets a tragedy in motion.

Simba hears a sound like thunder.
Dust rises, and the earth begins to tremble.
As he clings to a rotting tree,
a tide of wildebeests sweeps by.

Scar warns Mufasa of Simba's peril,
sending his brother charging
into the path of the stampede.

With his last reserve of strength,
Mufasa reaches up and places Simba on a ledge,
safe from the panicked herd.

Scrambling to save himself,
Mufasa sees his brother above him on the cliff,
stretching out a helping paw.

Inch by inch, Scar pulls Mufasa toward safety
but, at the last moment, lets him go and watches gleefully
as Mufasa vanishes beneath the slashing hooves.

In the stillness that follows,
Simba searches for his father
and finds a lifeless body sprawled in the dust.

As Simba sobs beside his father,
Scar savors his hour of victory.

Scar toys with Simba,
planting the seeds of guilt,
and tells the bewildered cub to flee
far from the Pride Lands.

With Scar's hyena mercenaries
in pursuit and gaining,
Simba plunges from a bluff
into the unknown.

The three hyenas watch
as Simba vanishes,
certain that the desert sun
will finish off their work.

Eloquent with false grief,
Scar reports the deaths of Simba and Mufasa
to the pride.

When the usurper's hyena cronies
lope into view,
the lionesses recoil in horror.

In his tree, Rafiki mourns
the loss of his friends.

Vultures circle overhead
as Simba collapses to the desert floor,
dazed by the blinding sun,
his legs too weak to carry on.

Eeeeeeeeeeeeeee–yaaaaaaaaaaaa!

With an earsplitting yell,
Timon the meerkat and Pumbaa the warthog
charge at the vultures.

As the ugly birds scatter,
the two friends see the lion cub
near death on the desert floor.

Timon pries Simba's lips apart
to reveal a fearsome set of teeth—
the jaws of a carnivore.

The cub seems so helpless;
Pumbaa picks him up
and carries him to the lush coolness
of the nearby jungle.

Waking in unfamiliar surroundings,
Simba thanks the Good Samaritans who saved him,
then rises to take his leave.

Persuading Simba to stay with them,
Timon and Pumbaa
introduce him to their philosophy:

HAKUNA MATATA—
No cares at all!

Timon pulls back a fern,
and Simba is introduced to his new friends' lair,
a jungle paradise complete with hanging vines,
a carpet of soft grasses, and a canopy of leaves.

Succulent spiders, juicy beetles, and worms—
Pumbaa and Timon initiate their newly found friend
into the surprises of their creepy-crawly diet.

And so it happens
that Simba, the lost crown prince,
grows to manhood . . .

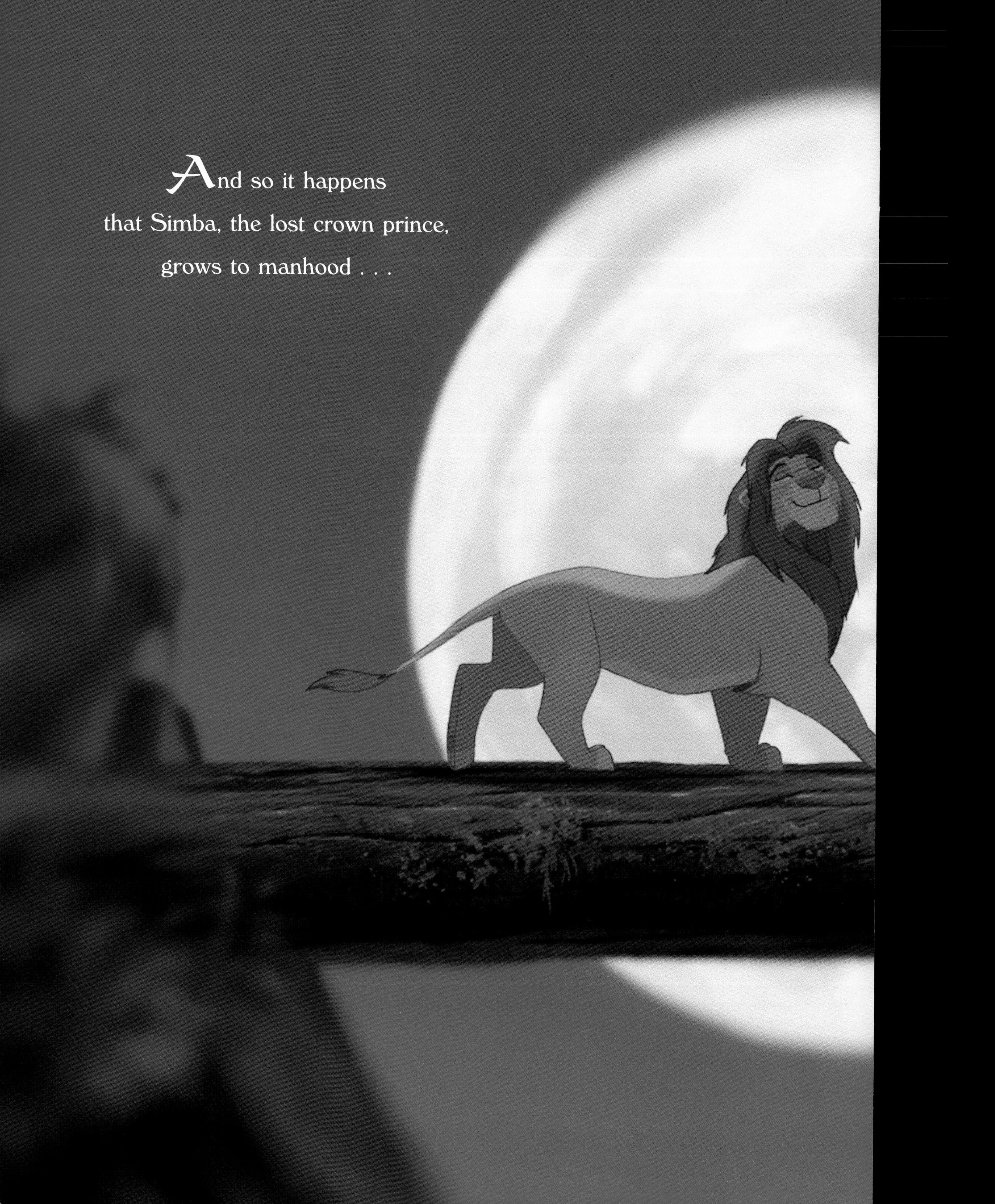

far from the Pride Lands,
in the jungle playground
of Pumbaa and Timon.

Meanwhile, at Pride Rock,
Scar the usurper sprawls in the royal cave,
tormenting Zazu to relieve his boredom.

Contemptuous and unannounced,
Shenzi, Banzai, and Ed burst into the royal presence,
demanding food. But the herds have moved on,
and the larder is bare.

One glorious tropical night,
Simba, Pumbaa, and Timon sprawl in a jungle clearing,
gazing at the stars.

Simba recalls another starry night
and his father's reassuring words.

Overcome by melancholy, Simba goes off by himself.
Flopping to the ground, he loosens seed floss
from a milkweed plant.

A breeze from the cooling plain below
lifts the seeds high into the starry sky
and carries them toward an ancient tree.

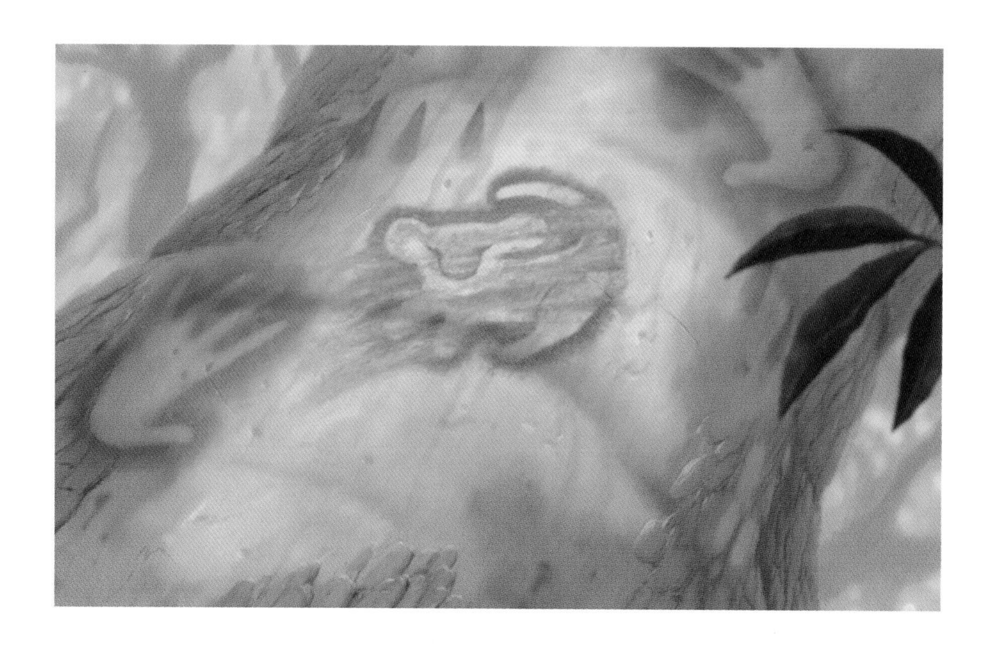

A hand snatches the seed floss from the air.
Rafiki sees what he has snared and dives into the tree.
In a big tortoiseshell, he mixes the floss
with the contents of a gourd,
interprets the signs in the gumbo, and laughs. . . .

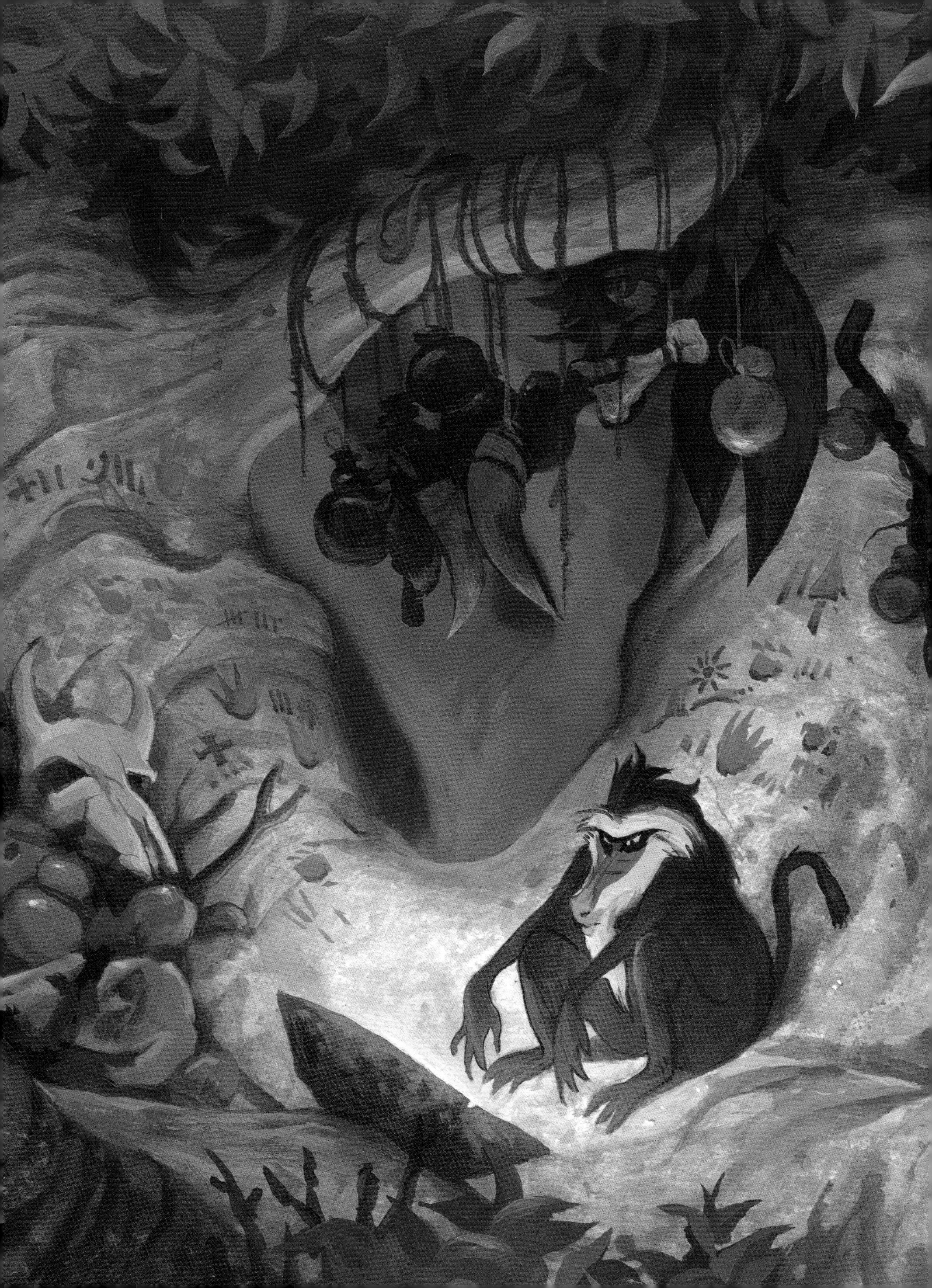

Simba is alive!

With all the stealth a warthog can muster,
Pumbaa stalks a plump and tasty bug.
Too late he spots a pair of hungry eyes.
The hunter is hunted.

The lioness springs at the trapped warthog
and all seems lost till, with a roar,
Simba dashes from the trees.

The lions battle in the dirt,
Simba gaining the upper hand until,
with a crafty flip, the lioness pins him.

Simba cannot believe that Nala has found him!
Nala cannot believe that Simba is alive!

Simba is still king.
This is Nala's firm belief—
a point of view that Simba does not share.

Together after so many years,
Simba and Nala feel the awakening of secret longings,
the reawakening of childhood dreams.

Simba and Nala wander through the enchanted landscape. Watching from afar, Timon senses the love between them and realizes that the carefree bachelor days have ended.

Nala tells Simba how Scar and his hyena hoodlums have laid waste to the Pride Lands.

Still Simba insists he will never return.

Confused by the news Nala has brought him,
Simba seeks solitude and guidance from the stars.

But the voices of the former kings are silent,
and soon his reverie is interrupted
by a curious song:

"Asante sana.
Squash banana.
We we nugu.
Mi mi apana."

Telling Simba that his father is alive,
Rafiki orders the bewildered lion to follow him.

Simba gazes into the waters of a pool
and sees the image of a full-grown lion there,
but it is merely his reflection.
Disappointment overcomes him once again,
but then he hears Mufasa's voice!

The darkness begins to shimmer.
Mufasa's spectral image appears,
an awesome presence filling the air with supernatural radiance,
as if some star has fallen to earth.

And now the phantom king
speaks to his son:

"Look inside yourself, Simba.
You will find that you are more
than what you have become.
You must take your place
in the Circle of Life. . . .

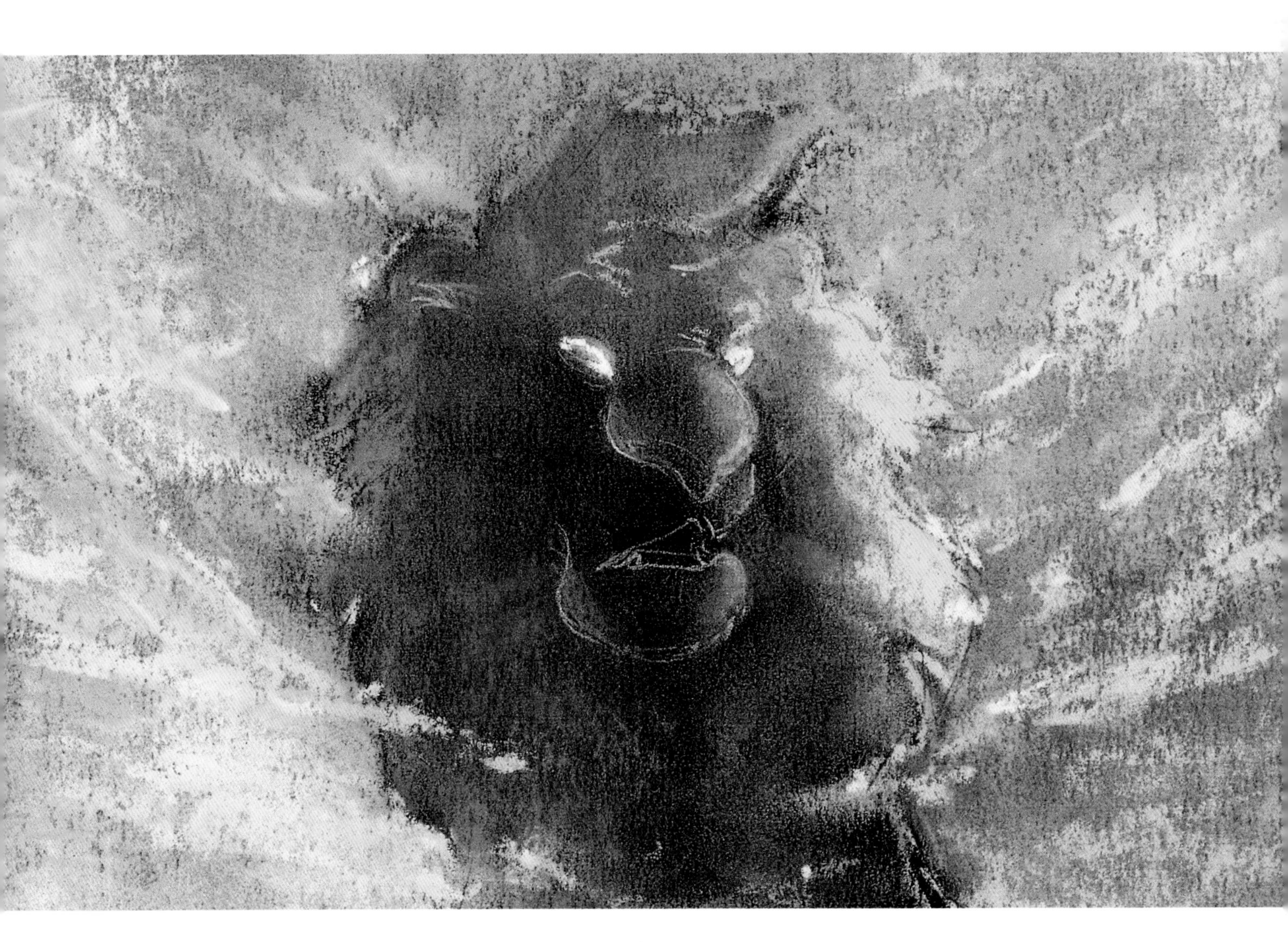

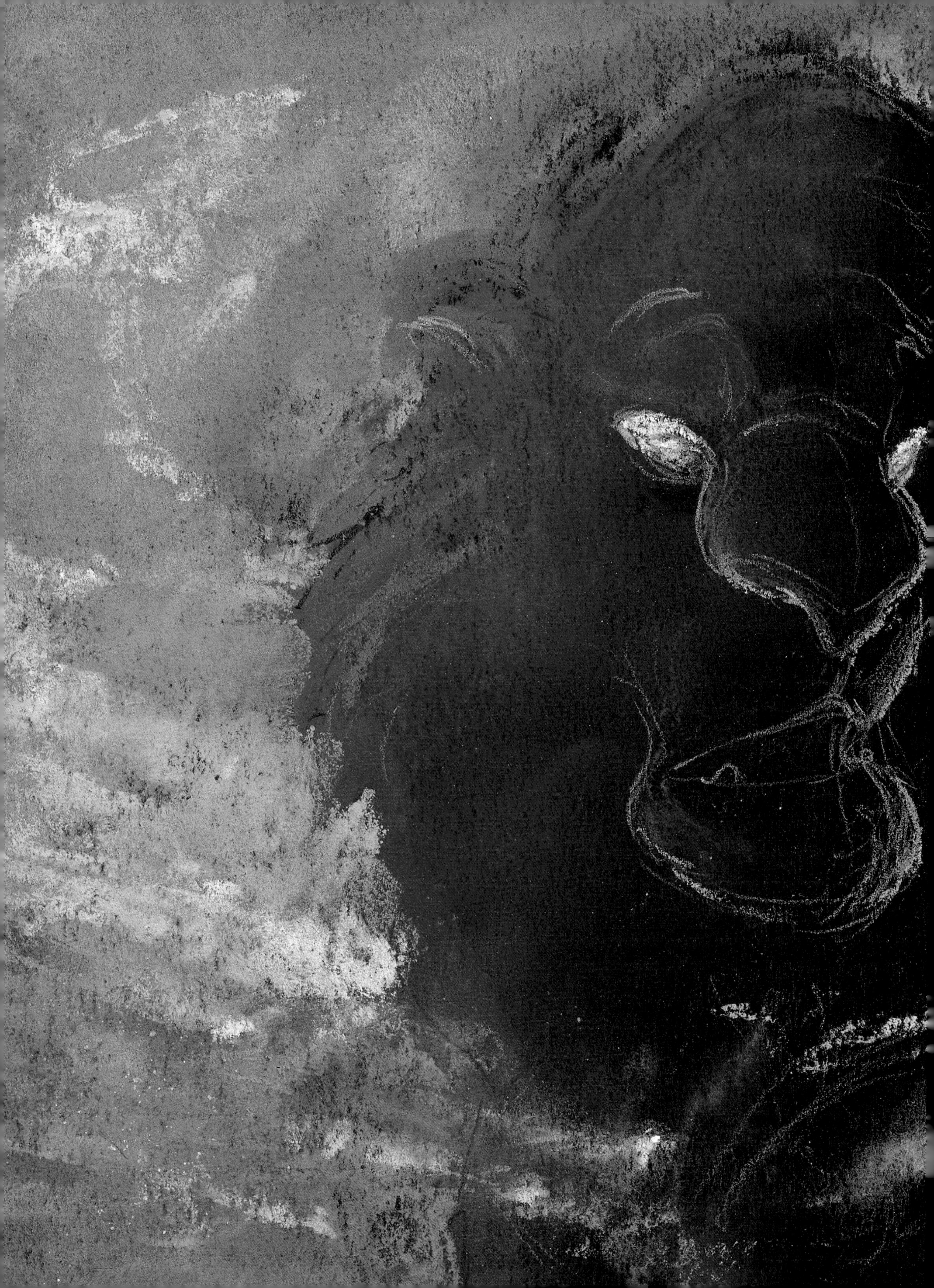

"Remember who you are."

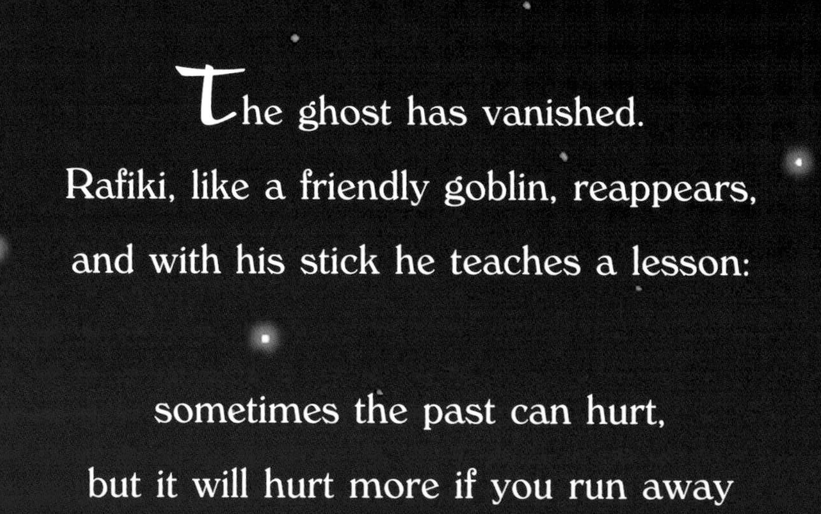

The ghost has vanished.
Rafiki, like a friendly goblin, reappears,
and with his stick he teaches a lesson:

sometimes the past can hurt,
but it will hurt more if you run away
than if you face its consequences.

Rafiki brings a message to Simba's friends:
the rightful king is on his way
to claim his throne.

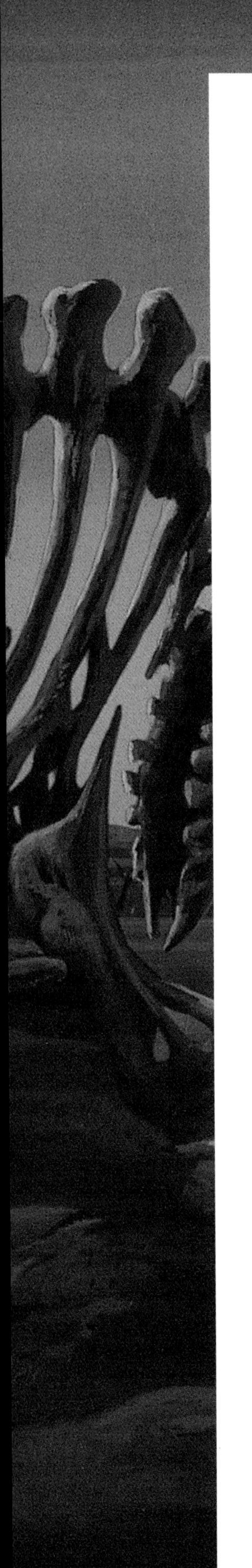

Simba speeds toward Pride Rock,
but when he reaches the borders of his kingdom,
he finds a scene of utter desolation—
naked trees, the earth scattered
with sun-bleached bones.

As storm clouds gather,
Nala arrives to fight at Simba's side—
Timon and Pumbaa too—
and together they move onward
to do whatever must be done.

At the foot of Pride Rock,
starving hyena sentries can't believe their eyes.
Pumbaa and Timon—
a banquet and a tasty snack—
ham it up, Hawaiian style.

From the cover of a boulder,
Simba and Nala watch
their friends' diversionary display, then—
while the sentries dream of chitterlings—
they dash toward Pride Rock.

As thunder rumbles all around,
Scar calls on Sarabi, Simba's mother,
demanding that her hunting parties
scour the land for food.

Flashes of lightning
set the bushes afire.
Flames throw Simba's noble head
and muscular body into silhouette.

For a moment, Scar panics,
believing Mufasa has returned to haunt him.

Simba nuzzles his mother,
assuring her that it is he,
back to fulfill his destiny.

Seeing that Simba, not Mufasa, is his foe,
Scar feels his confidence return.

Simba admits his past mistakes,
failing to notice that Scar has backed him up
against a precipice.

Simba slips and hangs from the rock,
seeming completely at Scar's mercy
just as Mufasa had been years before.
Gloating, Scar recalls Mufasa's death.

Murderer!

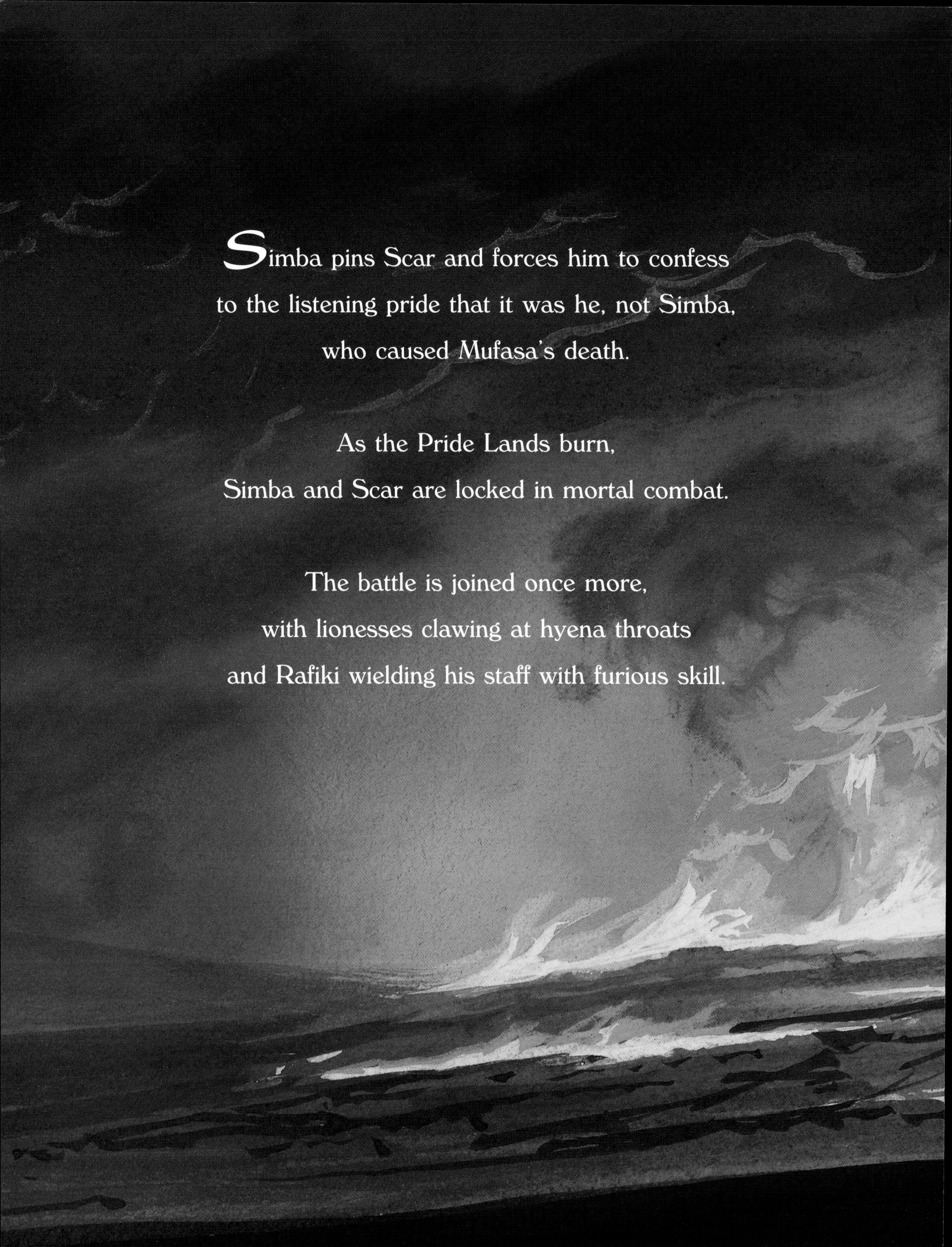

Simba pins Scar and forces him to confess
to the listening pride that it was he, not Simba,
who caused Mufasa's death.

As the Pride Lands burn,
Simba and Scar are locked in mortal combat.

The battle is joined once more,
with lionesses clawing at hyena throats
and Rafiki wielding his staff with furious skill.

To save himself, Scar lies again–
not realizing that his closest allies are listening
as he betrays them.

Giving his uncle one last chance, Simba tells Scar to flee.
Scar capitulates. Another trick.
Scar lunges at Simba once again,
but Simba sends his father's assassin flying off the ledge.

Scar lands in the burning brush,
Pride Rock at his back.
Led by Shenzi, hyenas advance upon him through the flames.
Friends, Scar calls them.
But they are friends no more.

Simba reunites with Nala and the pride,
and then, through smoke and rain,
Rafiki appears once more
and motions for the youthful king
to take his rightful place.

King at last, Simba climbs through the rain
to the summit of Pride Rock.

Simba looks up to the heavens once again
and sees the clouds part to reveal an ocean of stars.

Distant thunder rumbles,
and the new king hears the old king's voice:

"Remember!"

In answer, Simba lets out a mighty roar.

The Pride Lands return to life.
Tender shoots and sweet grasses
bring the great herds
back to the water hole,
and the union of Simba and Nala
brings a new cub into the world.

The sacred ceremony is repeated.
Rafiki holds the infant aloft for all to see,
and the world resounds
with song once more.

Index of Illustrations